The
Stand-In

The WindWriters

IndianGrass Books

ISBN:
ISBN-13: 978-0991659791
ISBN-10: 0991659791

"Lucy…. Lucy?"

I feel a hand resting gently upon my shoulder. It is warm and, like the voice calling my name, invitingly familiar.

"Luu-cy?"

I open my eyes and see her lips turn to a smile. "Good morning, dear." She reaches up and runs her fingers through my hair. "Do you know what day it is?"

Sleep's last fog disappears. I glance over and read my nightstand clock. 7:05 a.m. June 17, 2238. I yawn, return her smile, and reply. "It's my birthday."

"Not just any birthday," She says. "This is number fifteen, which means that you are ready. I have something for you."

My mother is the most tender person I know, but today that tenderness comes with something else. Her voice is quiet, more than usual; her eyes deeper, more than usual. There is a gentle intensity to everything about her and it makes me wonder. I adjust my pillow and sit up. From behind her back she produces the gift. I look at it. I do not understand.

"What is it?" I ask.

"It's a book…" She whispers.

"A book?" I mouth the words. I had heard about books, about paper, about pens and pencils, but until this moment had never seen any of these things. All I know is that I am not supposed to have them. **No one** is supposed to have them, and the idea that something this illegal is here, in my room, given as a gift by my own mother chills me. It has been decades since "The Emancipation", when libraries were stormed, every scrap of paper burned, and "possession" made a crime. Now each word, written and read is transmitted electronically. Composed on tablets and funneled through the FPA (Freedom Protection Agency), ideas are checked for accuracy and approved as "wholesome, true, right, and safe". But this. A book? A handwritten book??? Ideas? Unfiltered, off the grid, un-scrutinized, un-corrected ideas! I glance toward the window and see that the shade is pulled. Mother seems unaware of my nervousness and gently sets the gift on my lap.

Fear becomes curiosity. "This is paper…" I think to myself. I run my hands over it. The pages are weathered and tattered, the handwriting rough and faded. It smells old, musty, like the rotting shell of a tree fallen long ago. Except this is not the odor of decay or death. To me, it smells authentic, like it is the most real thing I have ever held.

"Paper."

I look up and find my mother's eyes. I have so many questions. "How old is it…a hundred years…two hundred…more? Who wrote it? Where did she get it? Why is she risking her life and mine like this?" Before I can open my mouth, she holds an upright index finger over her lips, nods, smiles again, and whispers.

"It's a very special book…"

For those who want to know....

December 2126

I cannot remember a time when we were free...

All I know is what my grandmother told me, that the day the Empire came to our land, was the darkest day in our history.

At the time, we were a strong people. Our country, Heiros, was a proud nation. Our cities were once beautiful, our land prosperous. For centuries, we followed the ways of our Ancient Writings, and listened for guidance from Dieu.

Dieu...
The Ancient Writings tell of a great leader who, from the beginning of time, had provided for us. Even now we believe that everything we have comes from him. Dieu appeared to

the ancients as an eagle, and when he left, he promised to send someone like him, another leader who, with kindness and compassion, would rule our land...

...But then came the empire.

At first, we fought them, but their army was too great. They destroyed our cities and burned our homes. So many of our people were put in prison. Some of us were killed

The rest now live in fear.

Our lives were once lived in freedom, but now we are slaves of the empire.

The Empire controls everything.

It started with 'The Gathering', when the police rounded up everyone and implanted tracking devices in our forearms. We use these chips to unlock doors, secure food rations, check in and out of work.   The Empire uses them to watch where we go and see who we are with.   If one of us is arrested, those who have been with the accused are also arrested. The Empire is everywhere. They control everything about us.

This is why I've written to you on paper. We cannot put this story on our writing pads. All electronically kept letters are monitored. Should the Empire see this, they would destroy the story and throw us in prison...So you must learn of these things in secret. Tell no one where it came from. Just read it, memorize it, and pass it along.

Someday what we tell in the dark can be shared in the light, but for now...

After they implanted their tracking devices, they forced us into the mines and the fields.

To this day,

they take our gold and silver.

They ship our coal and oil

to their capital.

They make us harvest our own grain but
give us only the smallest of rations, not
enough to feed our families.

They whip us.

They beat us.

They put us in prison

and very often for no reason at all...

Some of us die violent deaths.

Most of us starve.

Parents must divide a single loaf of bread between 8 or 9 people. Meanwhile citizens of the Empire live lavish lives. To us, the food that rots in their dumpsters looks like a banquet, but we are not invited, not even to their garbage pails.

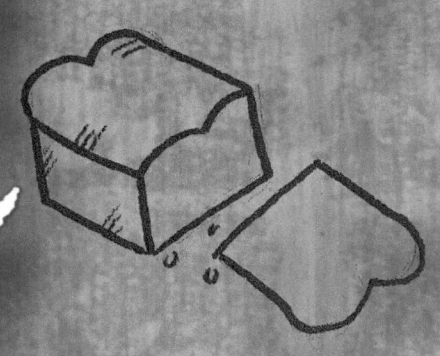

The Ancient Writings remind us of Dieu and his promise that someday soon one will come, one with special abilities. He will fight away invaders, bring us freedom, and make us a proud people again.

The Ancient Writings also tell of a New Heiros, a beautiful homeland off in the Great Beyond. In this place, there is no bloodshed, no war, no cruel empire. In this place, people are kind to one another.

To many, it sounds like fantasy, but most of us live with the hope that maybe there really is a Great Beyond, and maybe there really will be a

New Heiros, and maybe, just maybe the Ancient Writings are right and Dieu will send us such a leader...but for now we wait. We do not speak of these things. We do not share this hope with anyone else, for there is no one else who can be trusted.

So we live in fear,

   hold onto our secret dreams,

      and wait...

Even as we wait there is bloodshed.

Some among us fight a secret war.   They
call themselves The Resistance and they have
a single goal... make things impossible for the
empire. So they ambush empire police, and
sabotage supply lines.
If these rebels are discovered, The Empire
will hang them on the rack.
They risk their lives for a fight that is
unwinnable.

Others work with the Empire.

When the Empire first came, they needed people to run the cities and help keep the peace. Heiros' leading citizens were the perfect choice. These people were given privileges the rest of us didn't have.

In return, The Accomodators, as we have come to call them, work for The Empire. Don't get me wrong nobody likes the empire, but many Accomodators could see that when we resist, people get killed

So while most of the rest of us don't trust The Accomodators, they are a necessary part of our lives. They work with the empire to keep things calm, and thus minimize our suffering.

The rest of us, which is most of us, just keep our heads down.

We keep to ourselves, stay out of the way, and do what the Empire wants us to do. We hate the Empire and so wish to again be free, but for now the cost is too high.

The Resistance thinks that we are
cowards, but that's not it at all. We want
to stay alive for the day when we hope things
will change.
We are known as The Waiters because we
wait for the better times.
This is our world,

   dark,

      brutal

         and threatening,
and ever since the Empire conquered us,
   we have lived with this fear.

Then came CJ Ado...

He came from nowhere.

He was nobody.

He was not powerful.

He was not rich.

He didn't have any important titles.

He had no positions of influence.

CJ was a nobody who just traveled around

Hieros and made friends with other nobodies,

people just like him.

CJ Ado?
    He was a nobody...

    but he wouldn't be for long...

It didn't take us long to realize that CJ has special abilities.

He sees what no one else could see. He can look into a person's eyes and see their hurting soul.

He hears what no one else hears. He listens to silent cries, things that a person might think to themselves but never share with anyone else.

The things he sees and hears are invisible and unhearable to others, but for those who have such deeply buried troubles, they are absolutely real!

And only CJ sees these things.
And only CJ hears these things.

And then he reaches out, and when he
touches one of these hurting, crying people,
their loneliness, their loss, their trial, their
deep secrets are transferred on to him.

And it eases their hurt, and it soothes
their pain.
The last time such things happened,
was when Dieu walked among us...

Many of us wonder, "Who is CJ Ado?"
Of course, we never say such things aloud that would be dangerous.

Instead we just watch what's happening and wonder...

Where did he get these abilities? No one knows, not even CJ. I've heard that at first it scared even him, seeing total strangers who on the outside looked so normal, but deep within carried these hidden pains, struggles, and fears.

Yes, it scared him that he could see and hear so much. He told Mira, his mother, about it and she told him that she didn't know either, that for a long time she had seen these things in him but she didn't understand it either. "CJ," His mother said, "all I know is that there is so much hurt in the world I have to believe that you are here for a special purpose and that someday it will all make sense. Give it time, son. Give it time..."

CJ did give it time...

...and over time these abilities changed, became even stronger. It got so that he sees the pain, and feels the fear in anyone who was near, even in those who would call themselves his enemy.

Then CJ started teaching about the
Ancient Writings and what they meant.

He pointed to the skies and told stories of

Dreu. He spoke of a time when Heiros
would be new again, a time when leaders
would be compassionate, when they would love
and care for their people. He called upon
Hiros to show kindness, telling us to "Love
even those who hurt you, for a kindness
received warms the coldest of hearts."

Most of all, he spoke of a time when tyrants would leave and we would again be a proud people. He said "A new day is coming and you will be free of all that enslaves you!"

People crowded around
    to hear him say these things...
        People followed
            People listened
He told them...
"Rest from your troubles."
"Let me carry your burden"

"Know the kindness of Dieu, for he sees all that brings you down, and comforts you in your weakness."

They heard CJ say these things, and their hearts soared as though they were riding on Dieus' wings. They dared to believe that the Great Beyond and the New Heiros was not so far away, that it could be here.

It could be NOW!

This was HOPE....something that for generations had not been felt.

At first it was only whispered

"He sees my pain!"

"Could this be the one?"

"Is this nightmare finally over?"

Soon, however, this hope was so contagious

that not even the Empire could keep them

living in fear.

Others were getting nervous.

They wondered, "Who is this guy?"

"Doesn't he know he's playing with fire!"

Most of all, they realized the peril of such talk...for as anyone who has lived under tyrants knows, hope like this can have disastrous results.

One day a man approaches CJ. He is dressed in the clothes of a waiter but has never fit in with anyone. He is a loner, a drifter, and the people who know him stay away from him. He has no friends. Oh yes, some have tried to change that, but soon withdraw. This

man cannot keep friends, so he lives by himself,
and it is a lonely existence.

He approaches CJ. CJ has become wildly
popular and this man is VERY angry.
   There is a group of people surrounding CJ
and the man begins a verbal attack.

"Who do you think you are?

   What do you think you're doing?

You think you're something special, don't you! You think you're so important. Well let me tell you that you're nothing...

...NOTHING!!!"

The crowd around CJ is silenced. They want this man to go away. They want him to end this attack. CJ stops what he is doing, turns to the man, and places a hand on his shoulder. It is a soft touch. He looks into the man's eyes. As he speaks his voice is gentle.

"You're right, my friend, I am nothing. But you? You are very special. You are a rare gift, one of a kind and I see that. I know how you've been mistreated. I know how alone you feel. Stay with me and know that I want you to be my friend..."

The man is stunned. No one has ever talked to him like this. "Me special? Me a rare gift? Me???" He doesn't know what to say or do. CJ's kindness stops him cold. CJ's words change him.

It is night when Dr Nico comes to CJ.

He comes in darkness because he does not want anyone to see the two of them together. Nico is an Accommodator and wants to know more about CJ's special abilities. He wants to make a judgment about CJ, but as the conversation unfolds, it's clear that CJ is seeing into Dr Nico's heart.

This, of course, makes Nico afraid, interested, and most of all, wondering

"Who is this man?"

"Where did you come from?" Nico asks.

"Why do you want to know?

   Are you afraid?"

"I'm afraid people will get hurt."

"If we care about each other, no one will ever get hurt..." CJ pauses, then continues, "How about you, Dr Nico, there is so much fear in you.

So much anxiety... I feel it in your heart.
Don't be afraid, my friend   I care about
you."

Nico wonders, "How can he see this?" Then
he turns to CJ and says, "The Empire
won't understand this. They'll kill you!"
CJ smiles "They can't kill an idea They
 can't kill freedom so they can't kill me.
If they try everything lives on and gets
bigger.
    Hope gets larger.
       Freedom becomes so big

that no one will be able to stop it."

"I'm not kidding, CJ." Nico replies, "This is not a game! The Empire is powerful and dangerous. They will squash you and think nothing of it!!"

CJ puts a hand on Nico. "My friend there is something more powerful than the Empire, more powerful than their guns and tanks and police squadrons. It is the power of love and it overcomes everything else." CJ pauses, then continues,

"Rule people by fear and they'll comply. Motivate people with threats and they'll submit. But love them, care about them, give them your life, and you'll have their hearts. They'll willingly follow you anywhere..."

"Quiet CJ! Shush..." Nico's voice becomes a whisper. "This kind of talk will get you killed!"

"Kill me? If they kill me I'll come back in ways you cannot even begin to imagine!"

The next day, one of The
Accomodators and his wife
are walking down the street.
Their names are Jero and
Palla

Like all Accomodators, Jero
and Palla are well dressed. Like all
Accomodators they have money. Because they
are Accomodators, the Empire rewards them.
    They also have a good position in Hieros.
Jero works in Hieros' head city.

CJ approaches them and speaks to Palla

"Pardon me, madam, I believe I know you."

"Sir, we have never met."

"No, I know you. I can see inside and the hurt you carry with you every day. I know you have so many nice things, fine jewelry, lovely clothes, a beautiful home, but your heart is restless. I know of the child you lost. I know you. I can see you."

Jero chases CJ away, "Who do you think you are, talking to us like that? Leave my wife alone. Get out of here. GO!"

Then Jero turns to Palla, "What a Jerk!"

Palla agrees, "Some nerve he has, talking to us like that!"

...but inside Palla is thinking, wondering,

"That was 5 years ago.

I wonder how he knows about the baby?

I wonder how he sees my hurt?

I wonder..."

After this happens, Jero reports CJ to the Empire police. They start watching him. Jero sees CJ as a threat and a danger, not to the Empire but to his own people.

Accomodators are sometimes misunderstood. To most people, it looks as if Accomodators have sold out for their own gain. Some indeed have done just that, but not Jero. He cares about Hieros and the very fragile peacefulness in which they live. He sees the way people are gathering around CJ,

are following him, are talking about him as
the new hope and the one promised by the
Ancient Writings. Jero is worried that
maybe the empire will start cracking down
because people are gathering around a fellow
who gives them hope. Jero knows that hope
is dangerous, that hope is how people get killed

The Resistance has also been watching CJ
and they see an opportunity. They see the
groundswell of people. CJ's words have so
stirred the crowds that the Waiters and even

a few Accomodators are beginning to get restless. The time is ripe, talk of revolt is in the air and CJ is the perfect symbol for their cause.

"This CJ Ado is exactly what we need." They Say. "We will raise him up and make him our leader. It's our time, time to move against the empire!"

The Resistance gathers its weapons, secretly makes its plans.

CJ, of course, wants nothing to do with the Resistance and their hunger for bloodshed.

"Let the Empire have their guns," CJ teaches, "Do you want freedom? Then remember that every time you touch someone with compassion, you are more powerful than the mightiest of Empires, and you have made yourself free!"

As soon as he is finished speaking he approaches the captain of the Empire police.

"I know that your father just died. I can see that this is in your heart."

CJ touches the captain on the arm and the chief finds himself strangely at peace. He looks into CJ's eyes and wonders, "What just happened here?"

Instead of playing the part the Resistance plans for him, CJ reaches out, heals the heartache of those who oppress his people. He loves Hieros' most hated enemies.

The crowd has been watching this. CJ turns back to them and says, "For every drop of spilled empire blood, oceans of Hieros' blood will be your reward. Show kindness to those who enslave you. Care for those who beat and imprison you."

Of course, none of this matters. The crowds are already stirred. Revolution is in the air and, willing or not, the Resistance has their symbol.

Meanwhile Jero has been talking with many other Accomodators. They are all becoming nervous. They are afraid of the bloodshed that CJ's leadership would bring. "He is dangerous!" One of them exclaimed.

"Unfortunately I agree." Another nodded his head.

"We have to get rid of CJ Ado," Jero stated.

"But how?"

"We have to convince the Empire that he is a traitor."

That same week, the revolt begins. Breaking out all its weapons and rallying every rebel in Heiros, the resistance attacks!

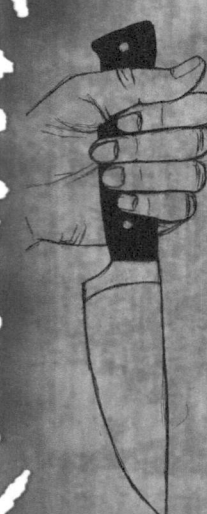

They are no match for the Empire and the rebellion quickly fails. Resistance Fighters, Waiters, even a few Accomodators are rounded up. The arrested number in the thousands and they are all scheduled to be executed!

Jero decides it is time and goes to Governor Gray, the Empire's local official.

Throughout the Empire, Gray has the reputation of being shrewd and brutal. The Empire calls him "The Keeper of the Peace".

Around here, he is known as "The Butcher of Heiros". In the last uprising, 25 years earlier, he sent 2000 rebels to the rack.

Now Jero comes to Gray and tells him that;

"The people have been misled by a radical named CJ Ado. Find him. Arrest him. Make him an example and force everyone you have just arrested to watch. Then, release them all. This will show your toughness and your mercy."

Gray listens carefully, thinking to himself, "We're dealing with dynamite here. Maybe this is a way to calm things down."

He sends a police squadron. In the dark of night, they surround CJ. His followers take out their knives and pain sticks and attack. The squadron of Empire 'Peace Keepers' is taken by surprise. One of them stumbles and falls to the ground. Two of CJ's followers grab his arms and hold him down. Another pulls out a knife and just as he is about to stab the man, CJ shouts, "Stop! Stop this Now!!!" CJ pushes the attackers aside and places himself between the Peace Keeper and his own followers. "If you stab him, you'll have to stab me first!"

His followers are dumfounded CJ turns to the officer, extends his hand, and pulls the man to his feet. "You will not be hurt. I promise you." He then turns to his followers. "Drop your knives. Drop your pain sticks. No one will be hurt. NO ONE!!!"

Now the squadron of Peace Keepers surround CJ. He is arrested, his hands bound with chains. His followers run away and hide.

CJ is immediately taken to Governor Gray. The leading Accomodators are standing with the Governor. Jero announces the charges,

"This is the man who inspired the revolt! He is dangerous to you and to us."

Gray turns to CJ, "Is this true?"

"Are you afraid of me too?" CJ replies.

Gray laughs. "Just answer the question."

"Don't be afraid" CJ whispers. "I want only to bring you peace."

It seems to Gray that CJ does not understand what is happening and that his life hangs in the balance. It seems to Gray that CJ isn't concerned about himself, or his fate, or anything. He looks at Jero and says,

"You're worried about this guy? He's just a nut job."

Jero's response is quick and pointed "I wonder, Governor Gray, what would the Emperor say if he knew you were being soft with a rebel, if he knew you weren't doing everything you could to keep the peace."

Gray's reply is just as sharp. "CJ Ado isn't a rebel, which is more than I can say for the rest of you... You should all die!"

Gray pauses, thinks, then turns again to Jero.

"So I suppose what you want is a Stand-In. You want this man to stand in for all the Rebels who should really die…"

Jero nods. "You're the Peace Keeper, right?"

Gray pauses again, and in that short silence CJ looks at him and says the strangest thing.

"I see your heart. Don't be afraid…"

It seems odd to Gray that this man should be so unconcerned about his own life. It also seems odd that CJ should be so right about what he is thinking. Gray pauses, looks directly into CJ's eyes and sees the deeply set compassion. It haunts him.

"I..." Gray pauses.

"I sentence you to The Rack!"

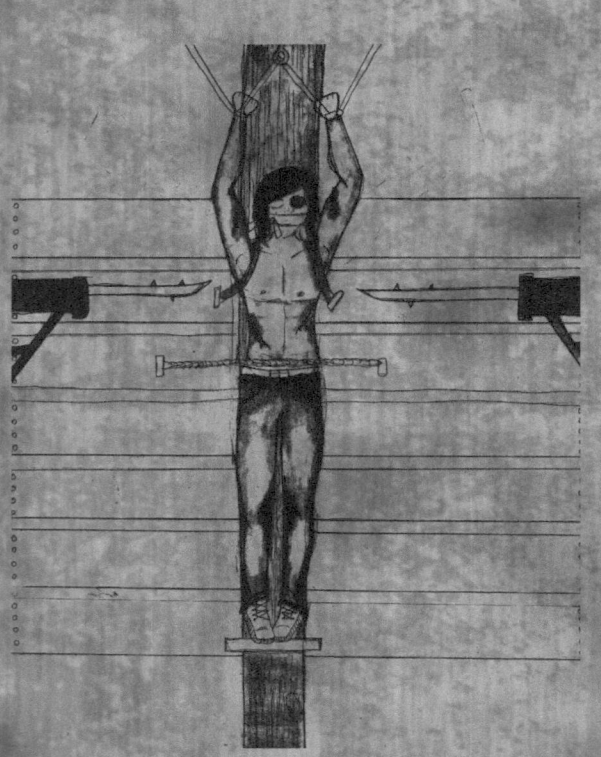

The Rack:

It is a painful and public death...

Chains are attached to CJ's wrist and ankles. The Police tighten the chains and stretch his body over the rack. Pain sticks are pressed against his arms, legs, and side. The sticks deliver an electrical shock that comes in waves.

The chains tighten.
    The shock intensifies then tapers off.
    The chains loosen.
    These waves come and go.

This torture can continue for hours and, in some cases, even days. With each execution, the people of Hieros are forced to watch.

The Empire uses The Rack as a deterrent. Everyone understands that rebellion means a painful and public death.

Those watching begin to shout.

"He should die."

"He tricked us into rebellion!"

"Traitor!" They cried

"Traitor against the Empire!!"

CJ is, of course, the only person in all of Hieros who is innocent, yet he alone is being put to death for the crime he did not commit.

Everyone is forced to watch. Most are content, even happy to let someone else take the blame. A few are not. They watch this gruesome execution and hate themselves for it...

CJ looks at them all...those who are happy for a Stand-In and those who are not.

"I love you."

His voice is weak and pain filled

"I will take this for you."

Those standing around the rack watch and

whisper among themselves..

"What did he say?"

   "He loves who?"

      "After what I've just done,

         he loves me?"

"I should be up there, not him..."

After his death, Jero and Governor Gray begin to worry that CJ's influence didn't die with him. They realize that should the Resistance discover the burial site, they'll turn it into a shrine. They will make CJ a symbol of hope that for generations to come will fuel rebellion's fires. Gray orders the Peace Keepers to secretly take CJ to the morgue, keep him there until morning, when he'll be cremated.

That night, the captain of the Peace Keepers covertly wheels CJ's body into Dr Nico's morgue. The only visible sign is a streak of blood that was left as CJ's lifeless hand brushed against the door frame.

Morning comes and the crematorium is ready. Nico approaches the guards and notices the now dried blood stain. The guard shrugs as Nico scans his wrist chip.

The scanner flashes green, signaling approval. Security, however, is tight. In addition to

Nico's tracking device, 2 key cards have been issued, one for Nico and one for the guard, the same guard who supervised CJ's arrival the night before. The men insert their key cards. With both keys in place, the seal breaks and the doors swing open. Dr. Nico and the captain walk into the room and stop in front of CJ's drawer. Just a few hours earlier, Nico supervised as CJ's body was wheeled into this very room and laid on the cold steel drawer. The drawer was then rolled into the vault and locked tight.

Now Nico unlocks that same door, and the captain pulls out the drawer.

"What in the..." Nico barely breaths the words.

"There's no way!" The captain chimes in.

"There's only one way in and one way out...double locked! I stood in front of this door all night long."

CJ is gone. He is just gone. The only thing left is the sheet that covered him, but CJ Ado is nowhere to be seen.

Both Nico and the guard are frozen. A dead

man locked in an exitless room...gone? What

is this? Where did he go? How did he

get out???

The captain of the Peace Keepers takes two

steps backward, and wonders what will happen

when Gray finds out?   Who will believe him?

But, of course, the question that raises

above all others is simply "Who? Who is this?"

Nico looks in the captain's eyes and sees the

the absolute terror that has seized him, for

https://www.facebook.com/thewindwriters

http://twitter.com/thewindwriters

http://instagram.com/thewindwriters

https://vine.co/u/1177452774972420096

ABOUT THE WINDWRITERS

The WindWriters are a very special group of young people. They are writers, artists, and idea people. They are social network gurus, publicity people, and designers. Most of all, The WindWriters are people who love the story. They hope you will read their book and take the journey.